Toffee Pockets

www.kidsatrandomhouse.co.uk

Toffee Pockets

Jeanne Willis
Illustrated by George Buchanan

RED FOX

TOFFEE POCKETS
A RED FOX BOOK 978 1 849 41489 0

First published in Great Britain by The Bodley Head, an imprint of Random House
Children's Books
A Random House Group Company

The Bodley Head edition published 1992
Red Fox edition published 1993

This edition published 2011

1 3 5 7 9 10 8 6 4 2

The Random House Group Limited supports The Forest Stewardship Council
(FSC),the leading international forest certification organisation. All our titles
that are printed on Greenpeace approved FSC certified paper carry the FSC
logo. Our paper procurement policy can be found at
www.randomhouse.co.uk/environment

Mixed Sources
Product group from well-managed
forests and other controlled sources
www.fsc.org Cert no. TT-COC-002139
© 1996 Forest Stewardship Council
FSC

Red Fox Books are published by Random House Children's Books,
61-63 Uxbridge Road, London W5 5SA

www.kidsatrandomhouse.co.uk

Addresses for companies within The Random House Group Limited can be found
at: www.randomhouse.co.uk/offices.htm

THE RANDOM HOUSE GROUP Limited Reg. No. 954009

A CIP catalogue record for this book is available from the British Library.

Printed and bound in the UK by CPI Mackays, Croydon

Contents

To F. G. Willis

Potting Shed

Packets of seeds,
Buckets of weeds,
Onions on a string
Bulbs in bowls,
A cure for moles,
A book on gardening.
Lots of pots,
Forget-Me-Nots,
Seedlings in a tray,
Trowels and spades,
Lawnmower blades,
And cans of greenfly spray.
Roots and shoots
And muddy boots,
Tomatoes turning red,
My favourite smell in all the world
Is Grandad's potting shed.

Pigeons

When I wake at Grandma's house
I hear the pigeons cooing.
Now every time I hear that sound
I wonder what she's doing.
I close my eyes and hear her voice
She says the same old words,
'Come on, sleepy head, get up,
It's time to feed the birds.'

Grandad's Hands

Grandad's got two big, kind hands,
One for Chrissie and one for me,
If we had another
Sister or brother,
God would have given him three.

Let's Play

Let's play skipping,
Let's play catch,
Let's have a rugby
Or a football match,
Let's throw bean-bags.
Let's climb a tree.
Grandma, I wish I had
Your energy.

The Face Inside the Frame

Grandad's got a photograph
Of him when he was small,
It doesn't really look like Grandad
Very much at all.
But Chrissie said that she was sure
The face inside the frame
Was Grandad's, and she pointed out
His smile was just the same.

14

A Joke and a Laugh

How does it feel to be really old?
Grandad says sometimes he feels the cold
And sometimes he feels a twinge of pain
Which pills cannot cure or a doctor explain.
Sometimes he finds he's a little bit slow.
He runs for a bus but his legs will not go.
He says it's his body that's letting him down
His face might be old but his heart doesn't
    frown.
There's nothing, he says, like a joke and a laugh
To make an old Grandad feel five and a half.

15

We Sing Rude Words

When Grandma makes us go to church
We giggle during prayers,
We sing rude word to all the hymns
And fidget on our chairs.
And when the vicar comes around
With money on a tray
We sometimes put our five pence in
And take ten pence away.

Fishing for Rainbows

The sky is grey.
We're fishing for rainbows
Today.

With nets on poles,
We're swishing the rainbow
Shoals.

Under the weed,
That's where the rainbows
Feed.

Rainbows in a jar,
Not sticklebacks. They're rainbows.
They are.

Sammy the Scarf

Grandad's scarf is called Sammy,
It says so on the back,
On a shiny, silky label
Stitched in swirly black.

I don't know what my scarf is called,
It has no label on.
It's such a shame it has no name,
I think I'll call it John.

Cabbage

Sometimes Grandma gives me things
I do not like to eat,
Cabbage leaves with soggy strings
And slimy luncheon meat.
I push them round and round the plate
And when she isn't looking
I stuff into my wellingtons
The worst of Grandma's cooking.

Funny Noises

Grandad drums his fingers on the table,
He makes a squeaky sound with sticky palms,
He makes a funny noise just like a raspberry
By blowing in the crooks of both his arms.
He whistles and he often taps his glasses,
He likes to rub his knuckles till they crack.
Grandma's always telling him to stop it.
Too late, we've learnt to make the noises back.

Old Fangled Things

Grandma hates new fangled things,
She much prefers her mangle,
She says that tumble dryers
Put her knickers in a tangle.
She hangs her stockings on the line
With lots of wooden pegs,
And when the wind blows hard, they look
Like rows of dancing legs.

The String Vest

Grandad wears a funny vest
It's made from holes and string,
It keeps him warm in winter
And it keeps him cool in spring.
He wears it when it's boiling hot
Refusing to undress,
He caught a vest-shaped suntan
When he sunbathed in Skegness.

Inside Our Dreams

Where do people go to when they die?
Somewhere down below or in the sky?
'I can't be sure,' said Grandad, 'but it seems,
They simply set up home inside our dreams.'

Fancy Dress Parade

There were prizes for the best fancy dress.
Chrissie was a rose fairy, with bright
Red roses in her auburn curls.
People said, 'She's the pretty one, out of the
  girls.'
People said, 'My, isn't she cute.'
But no one seemed to notice me,
The kid in the earwig suit.
No one, that is, except Grandad.
He knew and he understood
How the earwig felt, and he picked it up
And hugged it as hard as he could.

Monkey Nuts

Walking through the bluebell wood
With Barker off his lead,
If we stand very quietly
A squirrel comes to feed.
Grandad brings some monkey nuts,
We throw them on the ground,
Between the three of us we'll eat
A quarter of a pound.

Zanzibar

I found a caterpillar
I called him Zanzibar,
I gave him willow leaves to eat
And put him in a jar.
He wandered up and down his twig,
He ate and ate and ate,
I've never seen a caterpillar
Put on so much weight.
And then he seemed to shrink a bit
And off he went and hid.
He turned into a chrysalis
Beneath the jam-jar lid.
He slept for many days and nights,
When suddenly he stirred,
He stretched his wings and fluttered
Like a scarlet hummingbird.
I didn't want to let him go
But I heard Grandad say,
'When things grow up, like butterflies,
They have to fly away.'

Mixing Cocoa

Grandad's got a cocoa-mixing whisk.
Grandma isn't fond of it at all,
She'd rather that he used a spoon than risk
The cocoa powder sticking to the wall.

Before We Were Born

Sitting in our nighties toasting muffins on a fork,
It's really time to go to bed but we stay up
    and talk,
To Grandma and to Grandad till they both begin
    to yawn;
Stories that began before the two of us were
    born.

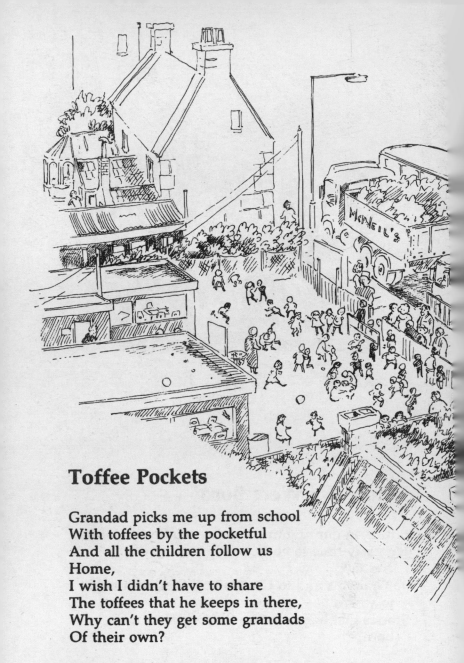

Toffee Pockets

Grandad picks me up from school
With toffees by the pocketful
And all the children follow us
Home,
I wish I didn't have to share
The toffees that he keeps in there,
Why can't they get some grandads
Of their own?

Tuck Your Vest In

Whenever I go round to Grandma's
She tells me to tuck in my vest.
She says that a person who lets it hang out
Cannot be considered well dressed.
She says that a person who won't tuck it in
Is asking to catch a bad cold
And a clip round the ear if she doesn't watch out.
So tuck your vest in, like you're told.

Polishing Grandad

Grandad's got no hair.
He's got a shiny head.
Because there's nothing
There to brush,
I polish him instead.

Name Tags

Grandma sewed my name in my blazer,
Grandma sewed my name in my shorts,
Grandma sewed my name in my beret and
  my coat
And the plimsolls that I wear for sports.
She said that it would stop me from losing
My bits and bobs, my satchel and my kit,
But I'm not the only Chrissie in the class
Which could be why these wellingtons don't fit.

Biscuit Problems

Grandma's got biscuits with faces,
Grandma's got biscuits that crunch,
And all sorts of chocolatey, jammery ones
You're not meant to eat before lunch.
There are boring ones in there for adults,
The brown ones with holes are the worst,
And those are the ones that I always end up with
For putting my fingers on first.

You Must Not Point

Grandma says we mustn't point
At people on the bus.
She says that certain passengers
Might think it rude of us.
No matter if their hats are strange
Or manners make us stare,
We're not to giggle, but pretend
The person isn't there.
And if we cannot help but laugh
Then just pretend to cough,
Or failing that, we'll stop the bus
And both of us get off.

Cricket

We fancied a game of cricket,
So Grandad made me a bat,
We never had stumps for the wicket,
Just peasticks, his braces and hat.
The ball was a piece of brown paper
Crumpled and tied up with string.
'The best things in life, pet,' said Grandad,
'Don't have to cost us a thing.'

Go To Bed

People who won't go to bed when they're told
Don't want to go to the zoo.
It's a bit of a shame, for there's monkeys and
   lions
And tigers and elephants too.
There are burger stalls, lollies and ice-cream
And a roundabout, swings and a slide,
And a grumpy old, humpy old camel
Who likes to give children a ride.
But a girl who won't go to her bedroom
And drop off to sleep right away,
Will be surely too tired in the morning
To go to the zoo for a day.
She'll be wanting to climb in her pushchair,
Or nod off to sleep by the bears.
'Do you want to go?' 'Yes, I do, Grandma!'
'Then jolly well get up those stairs.'

Shoes On

No one knows like Grandma knows
How hard it is to tie one's bows,
The more you try, the worse it goes
With laces.
The queen herself knows this is true,
The footman ties the royal shoe,
But even so, they still undo
In places.

Ghosts

Grandad says ghosts cannot hurt you,
Nobody can if they're dead,
And if ghosts exist
They're like hedgehogs,
Just night creatures searching for bread.

The Man in Brown

Grandma's got a photo of a man in brown.
She said he went to war.
I said I'd like to be a soldier too
But Grandma said, 'What for?'
I said I'd like to be a hero too,
And shoot all the baddies down.
'And kill someone's brother?' asked Grandma,
'Like they killed the man in brown?'
There's nothing to be gained by fighting,
There's plenty to lose, I'm sure.
It takes a coward to start a fight,
A hero to stop a war.

Greengages

We are down on our knees,
Chrissy, Grandad and I.
Planting greengage trees.
Three greengage stones
Which Chrissy, Grandad and I
Bury like Barker's bones.
'Whose will grow the tallest?
Grandad, we can't agree.'
'Promise to come back in ten years time,'
He said, 'and then we'll see.'

Hunting Bears

There's a spinney near Grandma's house
Where Barker hunts for bears.
At least, we think it's bears he hunts.
He may have even caught one once
And chased it up the stairs.
Whatever it was had great big paws,
Enormous, muddy ones.
It must have been a bear, Grandma,
I didn't eat your buns.

Tea with Aunty Mabel

If you ever go to tea with my Aunty Mabel,
Never put your elbows on the dining-room table,
Always wipe your shoes if you've been in the
  garden,
Don't ever burp. If you do, say pardon.
Don't put your feet on the new settee,
If she offers you a sugar lump, don't take three.
Don't dunk your biscuits, don't make crumbs,
Don't bite nails and don't suck thumbs.
Don't rock the budgie, don't tease the peke,
Speak when you're spoken to or else don't speak.
Do as you're told and if you're not able,
Don't go to tea with my Aunty Mabel.

Stabilisers

I had a bike with stabilisers on.
Chrissy took them off and now they've gone,
And so has all the skin on my chin and knees.
Have you got some plasters, Grandad, please?

Garden for the Blind

Me and Grandad often go
To the garden for the blind,
Which smells the sweetest,
The rose I can see?
Or the rose in the blind man's mind?

Paper Frogs

The best thing about having mumps
Was making a paper frog that jumps,
With Grandad by my bed.
Folding flap 'A' into flap 'B'
Is so much easier, you see,
When there's two of you instead.
The best thing about having mumps
Is you forget about the medicine and lumps
When Grandad's holding the spoon.
And he didn't mind about paint on the sheet
He bought me an ice-cream with sauce on to eat
I hope I get mumps again soon.

Foot Marching

Sometimes I stand on Grandad's feet
And he walks around the floor,
And he sings me ancient army songs
He picked up in the war.
Sometimes we go backwards,
And sometimes round-about,
I never, ever let him stop
Until he's worn me out.

Trafalgar Square

There are pigeons and pigeons and pigeons,
A Nelson and fountains that play
At the foot of some lions, magnificent lions
who stare in a stony-black way.
I wonder, if somebody lifted us up . . .
Would somebody be so kind
As to lift us both up on the lion's paws?
I'm sure that nobody would mind.

It's a wonderful view of Trafalgar Square
up near the lion's head.
'What can you see, girls?' called Grandma to us,
'Pigeons and pigeons,' we said.

Driving Grandad

Grandad can't stand aeroplanes
or modern cars, electric trains
or motorbikes. He doesn't mind a boat.
When Daddy takes him out, you know
He makes him drive the car so slow
The milk man overtakes us on his float.

Modelling Glue

Grandad isn't good with glue,
And sadly, nor am I,
I always drop it on my shoe,
He squirts it down his tie.
The model ship we tried to make
Was really rather poor,
Grandad made a slight mistake
And dropped it on the floor.
There must have been some glue about;
No matter how we tug,
The plastic sailors that fell out
Won't come off of the rug.

Cubby

Grandma has a lion cub
With worn-out ears and fur,
It once belonged to a little boy
Who used to live with her.
That little boy was my father,
It gives me such a thrill
To think that his kisses and cuddles
Are stuck to the lion cub still.

Cracker Hats

Daddy looks so silly in his tissue-paper crown,
Mummy's Christmas Cracker hat looks better
    upside down,
Chrissie's hat is far too big and Grandma's is
    too small,
Mine is stuck together wrong and doesn't
    fit at all.
But Grandad's hat, now there's a hat! It really
    looks a treat,
It sits so proudly on his head, its points all sharp
    and neat.
Daddy says it makes him look a bit like King
    Canute,
At least it did until he spilled that gravy down
    his suit.

The School Play

1. Today
   Is the school play
   I can't remember
     what
   I'm meant to say.

2. Grandad
   Helped me to
     rehearse
   The trouble is, I've
     gone from bad to
     worse

3. Standing
   In the wings
   With pixies, fairies,
     bumblebees
   And things.

4. Me?
   I'm a ladybird
   At least I think I
     was the last
   I heard.

5. Help
   I'm on the stage
   I've said a line from
   Mr Spider's Page.

6. Shall
   I carry on perhaps
   And listen out for
       boos
   or maybe claps?

7. Everyone
   Was really very
       kind.
   I'd got it wrong, but
   no one seemed
       to mind.

8. Except
   The spider, who
   without a word
   Came on stage and
       kicked
   The ladybird.

Monster Fighting

Grandad, get rid of the monster,
Grandad get rid of it quick.
It's hiding behind the big wardrobe,
Wallop it hard with your stick.
Now it's gone under the table.
Now it's gone over the chair.
After it, Grandad! just hit it,
Just hit it and stop saying 'where?'
'Got him! I've got him,' cried Grandad,
Waving his stick in the air.
We hadn't the courage to tell him
The monster had never been there.

Larder Raid

Grandad, Grandad, let's have a larder-raid,
Let's have a larder raid, I'm hungry after class.
Let's fetch orange juice, banana shake and
    lemonade,
Let's fetch ice-cream and whisk it in a glass.
You cut the bread up, I'll fetch the filling,
I'll fetch the filling, and mix it with my fork.
I'll make the sandwiches and you can do the
    grilling,
I'll fetch the ginger ale and you pull out the
    cork.
How about a fairy cake? Some squashy cubes
    of jelly?
Little cubes of jelly can be lovely when they're
    raw.
We'll go and eat our feast and watch Blue Peter
    on the telly,
Sitting on some cushions in the middle of
    the floor.

All rolled up,

All rolled up and done around with ribbon,
Red ribbon, rolled up and all done around.
Faded writing on tissue-thin paper,
What's this, Grandma? What have we found?
All soft-scented, kept like treasure,
Ancient envelope, sealed with a kiss.
Secret scribbling sent by a soldier?
Grandma, Grandma, what's all this?
All bright-eyed and somehow bashful,
Grandma says, 'I'll take those please,
Best not to play with them, rather precious,
Best not to play with memories.'

Jonathan J

There'a horrible schoolboy called Jonathan J
who chases me home down the lane
with his umbrella handle hooked on to the belt
of the mac that I wear in the rain.
'Off with you, off with you Jonathan J,'
I shout, but he does it again.
And I try to escape but he charges behind
like a terrible, run-away train.
I mentioned to Grandad how horrid he was
And asked him to chase him away.
'He's in love with you,' Grandad said. 'Give him
   a chance,
Attaboy, Jonathan J.'